Lara
the Black Cat
Fairy

Special thanks to Narinder Dhami

ISBN 978-0-545-42596-4

Copyright © 2009 by Rainbow Magic Limited.

All rights reserved. Published by Scholastic Inc., 557 Broadway, New York, NY 10012, by arrangement with Rainbow Magic Limited.

12 11 10 9 8 7 6 5 4 3 2   12 13 14 15 16 17/0

Printed in the U.S.A.   40

First Scholastic printing, February 2012

Lara
the Black Cat
Fairy

by Daisy Meadows

SCHOLASTIC INC.

New York   Toronto   London   Auckland
Sydney   Mexico City   New Delhi   Hong Kong

There are seven special animals,
Who live in Fairyland.
They use their magic powers
To help others where they can.

A dragon, black cat, phoenix,
A seahorse, and snow swan, too,
A unicorn and ice bear —
I know just what to do.

I'll lock them in my castle
And never let them out.
The world will turn more miserable,
Of that, I have no doubt!

Contents

North, South, East, West

"Come on, Kirsty." Rachel Walker picked up her backpack and smiled at her best friend, Kirsty Tate. "It's time for our next activity—we're going on an orienteering expedition."

"Oh, great!" Kirsty exclaimed happily, lacing up her hiking boots. "I'm really looking forward to it." Then she grinned. "But, to be honest, I'm not exactly sure what an orienteering expedition is!"

Rachel and the other girls in the cabin—Emma, Natasha, Katie, and Catherine—smiled sweetly at Kirsty.

"Orienteering is when you use a compass and a map to find your way to a specific place," Emma explained. "All the different teams try to get there first. It's a lot of fun."

"It sounds fantastic," Kirsty agreed.

"I've enjoyed all the camp activities so far," Rachel remarked to Kirsty as their bunkmates went outside.

Kirsty nodded. "And it's been even *more* exciting since our fairy friends asked us for help!" she whispered.

On the day the girls arrived at the camp, they discovered that Jack Frost had been up to his old tricks again in Fairyland. This time he and his goblins had kidnapped seven magical animals from the Magical Animal Fairies.

The magical animals were very rare because they helped spread the kind of magic that every human and fairy could possess—the magic of imagination, luck, humor, friendship, compassion, healing, and courage. The fairies trained the magical animals for a whole year to make sure the animals knew how to use their powers. Then they could spread their wonderful gifts throughout the human and the fairy worlds!

But Jack Frost was determined to keep the animals from using their magic gifts. He wanted everyone to be as grumpy and miserable as he was! So he and his goblins had stolen the young magical animals and taken them to his Ice Castle. But the animals had managed to escape into the human world, where they were now hiding. Of course, Jack Frost sent his goblins after them, but Rachel and Kirsty were determined to find the young animals first and return them safely to Fairyland. The girls knew they could count on the Magical Animal Fairies for help.

"I'm glad we found Sizzle the dragon yesterday," Rachel said, as she and Kirsty left the cabin. "Ashley was so happy to see him again, wasn't she?"

Kirsty nodded. "I hope we find the other animals soon," she said anxiously. "Remember what the fairies told us—the magical animals can't always control their powers because they haven't finished their training yet."

"But they really tricked Jack Frost and his goblins when they escaped from the Ice Castle, didn't they?" Rachel laughed.

Rachel and Kirsty joined their bunkmates, who were standing with the girls 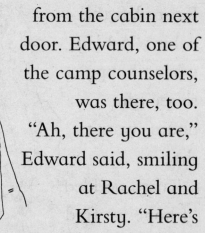 from the cabin next door. Edward, one of the camp counselors, was there, too. "Ah, there you are," Edward said, smiling at Rachel and Kirsty. "Here's your map and compass. Now, you're all going to walk due west for twenty-seven paces, and then you'll find your mystery location!"

Everyone listened carefully as Edward explained how to place the compass on the map and watch the magnetic needle to find out which direction was north.

"Hold the map steady, Kirsty," said Rachel as the needle swung around. "Look, that's north."

"So west is *that* way," Kirsty said,

pointing to her left. "Come on, Rachel!"

Some of the other campers had already headed in that direction, and Rachel and Kirsty followed them, counting each step under their breaths.

"Twenty-four, twenty-five," Rachel murmured. Then she stopped and burst

out laughing. "Look, Kirsty, we're at the Mess Hall!"

"Nice work, everyone," called Edward as he hurried out of the Mess Hall. He began handing out bottles of water and granola bars. "That was easy, wasn't it? Now we're going into the field to try a longer route, so follow me!"

Edward strode off and everyone rushed after him. Soon they were out in the fields that surrounded the camp.

"In orienteering, it's really important to use your compass correctly," Edward explained, opening the gate into the field. "Because this is a race between different teams, you need to find the shortest route between the points on your map. If you don't, you won't win!"

"I'm enjoying this, aren't you, Rachel?" Kirsty remarked, taking a sip of water. "I never thought maps and compasses could be so much fun!"

Rachel was about to reply when a soft, muffled noise suddenly caught her attention. She stopped and cocked her head to one side.

Meow! There it was again!

"I can hear a cat," Kirsty said, glancing around at the long grass.

"Me, too," Catherine agreed.

Suddenly, Rachel noticed a tiny, jet-black cat in a patch of fuzzy dandelions. The cat was batting at the plants and chasing the fluffy white seedlings as they floated off into the air.

"Look, there it is," she pointed out. "Isn't it cute? I wonder where it came from."

"It's probably from one of the farms," Edward replied. "There are a lot close by."

"Oh, I love cats," Natasha said eagerly. She knelt down on the grass and held out her hand. "Here, kitty!" she cooed.

The cat stopped playing and looked over at the group. She had beautiful, emerald-green eyes and her black fur gleamed in the sunshine. As the cat began to purr loudly, Kirsty gave a gasp.

"Rachel!" she whispered. "The cat's whiskers are shimmering!"

"I know, I can see it, too!" Rachel murmured, her heart thumping with excitement. "It must be fairy magic!"

Before the girls could say anything more, Rachel suddenly felt her gold locket slip from her neck. She made a grab for it but missed, and it fell into a shallow ditch at her feet.

"Is it broken?" asked Kirsty as Rachel bent to pick it up.

Rachel examined the clasp and shook her head. "No,  it must have just come undone, somehow," she replied, frowning.

At that moment, a loud flapping of wings overhead made everyone look up. A large pigeon was swooping down toward them. Its bright eyes were fixed on the half-eaten granola bar in Catherine's hand.

"Help!" Catherine shrieked in alarm, as the pigeon grabbed the bar and flew off.

"Are you OK, Catherine?" asked Rachel. Before Catherine could reply, Natasha, who was still kneeling near the cat, gave a cry of pain.

"Oh, my hand's itching!" She gasped, rubbing it hard. "I must have touched that patch of poison ivy—" She pointed to a patch of leaves with reddish stems. "But that's weird. I don't remember seeing it before!"

"Here." Edward pulled a tube of cream from his bag and passed it to Natasha. "Rub this where it itches, and it will feel better."

"Rachel, have you noticed that *three* unlucky things happened in the last minute?" Kirsty whispered to her friend. "This little black cat *must* be one of the missing magical animals!"

Buttercup Surprise

Rachel nodded. "We know that one of the missing magical animals is a black cat who's being trained to spread good luck," she agreed. "And we also know that because the animals are so young, their magic is very unpredictable."

"In this case, it's working in reverse!" Kirsty murmured. "We're getting bad luck instead of good luck!"

17

"We'd better take the cat back to
Fairyland before any goblins appear,"
said Rachel. She turned to look at the
cat again, but at that very moment, it
raced off, bounding through a patch of
red poppies. Rachel and Kirsty shared a
glance of dismay.

"OK, that little cat's got the right idea!" Edward announced, clapping his hands. "Let's get a move on."

"At least Edward and the other girls haven't noticed anything out of the ordinary about the cat," Kirsty whispered. "They think it's just a farm cat."

Meanwhile, Edward had begun dividing the girls into teams of two.

"Rachel and Kirsty, you're a team," he said, handing them an envelope.

"Oh, that's good!" Rachel exclaimed in a low voice, grinning at Kirsty. "We'll be able to keep a lookout for the cat."

"Yes, maybe we're getting a little bit of good luck, too!" Kirsty pointed out.

"OK, each team has a different set of instructions inside their envelope," Edward explained. "The clues will lead you all around the fields, but if you have any problems, I'll be close by." He glanced at his watch. "It's noon now. We should aim to meet up again around 12:30. All the instructions will lead you to the same place, where there will be a surprise waiting for you! Good luck!"

"I wonder what the surprise is," Kirsty remarked, tearing open the envelope.

She unfolded the instructions and read aloud: "'Head north through the field for sixty paces until you reach a fence. Then turn right (due east). Follow the fence for ten paces until you reach a wooden gate.'"

"That doesn't seem too difficult," Rachel said, as the other teams began to hurry off in different directions. "Maybe we'll spot the cat again while we're following the instructions!"

"I hope so," Kirsty replied.

Carefully, the girls lined up the compass and began to walk north, counting their steps. As they walked, they both scanned the field. There was no sign of the little black cat.

"Twenty-one, twenty-two," Kirsty murmured. Then she stopped. "Rachel, was it fifty or sixty paces to the north?"

"I can't remember." Rachel shook her head. "Can you check the paper, Kirsty?"

Kirsty unfolded the instructions again. Then she let out a gasp.

"Rachel, look!" she cried. "The writing has changed—and so have the directions!"

The girls stared at the paper. Now there were swirly golden letters that read, "Head west for forty strides until you find a cluster of glimmering buttercups."

"Fairy magic!" Rachel gasped. "It must be! Quick, Kirsty, which way is west?"

Trembling with excitement, Kirsty looked at the compass.

"That way!" she said, pointing across the field.

The girls hurried west, counting their paces as they went.

"Look at that golden light!" Kirsty pointed up ahead after they'd gone thirty-eight paces. "That must be the patch of buttercups glimmering in the sun."

"I wonder what we'll find there?" Rachel said eagerly.

The gold buttercup blooms were
nodding and dancing in the warm
breeze. Rachel and Kirsty bent over the
flowers, peering down at them. Suddenly
Rachel clutched Kirsty's arm.

"Look, Kirsty!" she exclaimed.
"Right there, in the middle of all the
buttercups!"

Kirsty looked
where Rachel
was pointing
and saw a
tiny fairy
perched on
a buttercup,
waving up at them.

"It's Lara the
Black Cat Fairy!" Kirsty cried.

A Trail of Clover

Looking very happy to see Rachel and Kirsty, Lara fluttered up out of the buttercups. She wore a silver cardigan, jeans, black buckled boots, and a scarf printed with little cats. Her long, shiny black hair swirled around her as she flew to land gracefully on Kirsty's shoulder.

"Hello, girls," Lara said with a big smile. "I'm so glad you got my message! I'm looking for my little black cat, Lucky. I just know she's close by!"

"We saw her a few minutes ago, Lara," Rachel explained quickly, "playing in a patch of dandelions."

"But she ran away before we could catch her," Kirsty added.

Lara nodded. "We have to find her before Jack Frost's goblins do," she said anxiously. "We'd better search the fields. Which way do you think we should go first?"

Rachel and Kirsty glanced around.
The other teams had scattered now, and
there weren't any other campers nearby.

"Maybe we should go back to the
dandelion patch and start from there,"
Kirsty suggested.

Rachel was about to agree, when she
looked down and noticed something that
made her eyes open wide with surprise.
There, nestled in the grass at her feet,
was a four-leaf clover.
As Rachel stared
down at it, excitement
flooded through her.
She'd heard about
lucky four-leaf clovers
before, but she'd never
seen one. They were very rare!

But then Rachel blinked in surprise as

she noticed *another* four-leaf clover close
to the first one—and then another, and
another!

"Look!" Rachel gasped, kneeling
down and pointing at the little plant
right in front of her. "I think I found a
trail of four-leaf clovers!"

"Wow!" Kirsty gasped. "I've never
even seen *one* before—never mind a
whole trail!"

Lara was clapping her hands in

delight. "I bet Lucky left this trail!" she declared. "We should follow it right away!"

Quickly, Rachel and Kirsty began to follow the winding trail of four-leaf clovers. They were easy to spot in the grass because they shimmered with fairy magic.

"The trail seems to lead us in the direction of that farmyard over there," Kirsty said, pointing ahead of them.

The farmyard looked very quiet. There was no one around—just a few geese waddling here and there. Lara and the girls could also see a big barn and three haystacks.

"The trail ends here," Lara said with a frown, pausing at the edge of the farmyard. "But Lucky's still around here somewhere. I can definitely sense that she's close by!"

"Let's search the farmyard," Kirsty suggested, glancing at Rachel. But her friend was frowning and looking confused.

"What's the matter, Rachel?" asked Kirsty.

"I'm sure that there were *three* haystacks in the farmyard a moment ago," Rachel replied. "But look." She pointed across the yard. "Now there are only two!"

Kirsty and Lara stared at the haystacks. Rachel was right. There were only two of them now.

"That's strange—" Kirsty began.

Suddenly they all heard a tiny *meow*. The next moment, a small black cat

bounded across the farmyard, chasing
a leaf that danced in the
breeze.

"Lucky!" Lara cried out.

Lucky stopped in front of one of the
haystacks and eagerly cocked her head
at the sound of Lara's voice.

"Lucky!" Lara called again.

At that very moment, a long green
nose poked out of the middle of the
biggest haystack. Then a second
nose poked out of the other one.

Rachel, Kirsty, and Lara watched
in horror as one pair of green arms,
and then another, popped out of the
haystacks.

"Goblins!" Kirsty exclaimed. "They're
hiding in the haystacks!"

As Lucky turned to run toward Lara,
the goblins leaped out of the haystacks.
One of them grabbed Lucky! The cat
meowed and wriggled, but couldn't get
away. Chuckling triumphantly, the
goblins scurried across the farmyard.

"After them!" Lara cried.

Three Against Three

Immediately, Kirsty and Rachel ran
after the goblins, with Lara flying
alongside them. But as they dashed
across the farmyard, the third haystack
suddenly appeared from around the
corner of the farmhouse. It stopped in
front of them and blocked their path.

"Oh, no!" Rachel groaned, skidding to a halt. "That's the other haystack!"

"Haystacks don't move on their own," Kirsty said. "There's a goblin inside!"

"Don't worry, girls!" Lara declared, flicking her wand and sending fairy sparkles dancing around them. "We'll fly over it!"

Instantly, Kirsty and Rachel shrank down to become as tiny as Lara, with sheer, sparkly wings on their backs. All three of them whirled up into the air and flew over the top of the haystack.

"No fair!" the goblin inside shouted grumpily.

Rachel glanced back over her shoulder. "He's coming after us," she warned. Sure enough, the goblin shook himself free of the hay and charged across the farmyard behind them.

"I think those other two goblins are heading for the barn," Kirsty panted.

The three friends flew as fast as they could. Soon, they began to catch up with the two goblins in front of them.

Then the goblin holding Lucky gave a

loud roar of surprise as he tripped over
a milk pail that was lying in the middle
of the farmyard. The pail flew up into
the air and landed right on the goblin's
head!

"Help!" he
shouted, stumbling
around. "Who
turned out the
lights?"

"This might be
our chance to grab
Lucky!" Lara
whispered to Kirsty and
Rachel.

But the other goblin was too quick for
them. Leaving his friend stuck in the
milk pail, he grabbed the little black cat
from him and rushed toward the barn.

But he didn't notice a patch of grain
that had been spilled near the barn door.
As he slipped and
landed on his
bottom with a
shriek, he
accidentally let
go of Lucky.

"The goblins are
having lots of bad luck!" Rachel
whispered. She, Lara, and Kirsty flew
down toward the kitten. "Let's grab
Lucky and get out of here!"

Before they could reach the little cat,
the first goblin finally pulled the milk
pail from his head. He darted toward
the barn, scooped up Lucky, and ran
inside, slamming the heavy door shut
behind him. Meanwhile, the other

goblin was still sitting on the ground, groaning.

"Look out!" shouted the third goblin, who was chasing after Lara, Kirsty, and Rachel. "Pesky fairies!"

The goblin who had slipped glanced up and shrieked with rage. He jumped to his feet and began swatting at Lara and the girls as they hovered near the barn door.

"We have to find a way into the barn!" Lara yelled as both goblins jumped up and down, trying to knock the fairies out of the air.

"Let's take a look around," Kirsty

suggested, dodging the goblins' big, green hands.

Lara, Rachel, and Kirsty slowly circled the barn, keeping well out of reach of the two goblins below.

"Look, there's a crack in the wall!" Rachel said eagerly. "Do you think it's big enough for us to get through?"

"Sure it is!" Lara grinned. "Come on!"

She flew forward and slipped through the crack. Rachel and Kirsty followed.

The barn was full of sacks of animal feed and farmyard tools. Kirsty glanced around and noticed a big tabby cat sleeping peacefully at the back of the barn on a small pile of hay.

Meanwhile, the goblin was perched on a large sack of animal feed, still holding Lucky. He was stroking her head gently.

"Well, at least he's being sweet to poor little Lucky," Lara whispered to Rachel and Kirsty. "What should we do now, girls? We need a plan!"

Suddenly there was a loud knock at the barn door.

"Let us in!" screeched one of the
goblins outside. "Three of those
annoying fairies just flew into the barn.
They want our magic cat!"

"Oh, no!" Rachel groaned
under her breath.
The goblin holding
Lucky looked up and
scowled as he saw Lara
and the girls fluttering
overhead. Clutching
the cat tightly, he
rushed over to the
door and let his
friends into the barn.
"Ha, ha, ha!" chuckled
the third goblin
triumphantly. "Now
it's three against three!"

Lucky meowed anxiously, gazing helplessly at Lara and the girls with her big, emerald eyes.

"What are we going to do?" Rachel whispered.

Kirsty thought hard. How were they going to get Lucky away from the goblins and escape? She glanced around the barn for inspiration and noticed that the tabby cat had woken up and was watching them all with interest.

Suddenly, Kirsty had an idea!

Double Bad Luck

"Lara!" Kirsty murmured quietly. "Could you turn the barn cat over there into a black cat, just like Lucky?"

"Of course!" Lara nodded.

"And can you please make me and Rachel our normal size again?" Kirsty added.

"In no time!" Lara replied, her eyes twinkling. Hovering behind the girls so that the goblins couldn't see what she was doing, Lara pointed her wand at the tabby cat and sent a stream of fairy sparkles toward it. Rachel's eyes widened as she saw the tabby's coat turn a gleaming jet black, just like Lucky's.

"Well, the cat doesn't seem to mind!" she whispered to Kirsty as the cat busily began to groom herself. "I think I guessed what your plan is, Kirsty!"

"Let's hope it works," Kirsty said under her breath.

With another wave of Lara's wand, the girls grew back to their human size. The goblin holding Lucky glared at them and took a step backward. Immediately, the other two rushed forward, shielding him from Lara and the girls.

Kirsty ignored them. She walked to the back of the barn and picked up the newly black cat. The cat was very friendly and nestled down in Kirsty's arms, purring happily.

"Look, Rachel," Kirsty said, "we found a *new* lucky cat!"

Rachel nodded. "Yes, and look how big it is," she replied. "That means our cat is *much* luckier than that little cat the silly goblins have!"

The goblin holding Lucky and the haystack goblin looked at each other in dismay. Then they both stared at the barn cat in Kirsty's arms, looking very envious.

"No, no, NO!" the third goblin announced loudly, hands on hips. "There's no way we're falling for that old trick again!"

Kirsty and Rachel exchanged a worried glance.

"We *always* end up swapping something magical for something useless," the goblin went on. "We're not swapping this time, so go away! We're taking this magical animal straight back to Jack Frost!"

"Girls, we can't let them leave!" Lara whispered.

Rachel and Kirsty ran forward to grab Lucky, but the goblins had already scooted away. Dodging the girls, they ducked under a ladder that was leaning against the wall and headed for the barn door.

At that moment, an idea popped into Rachel's head.

"Oh!" She let out a loud gasp of horror. "I can't believe you just did that! You ran under a ladder, holding a black cat!"

The goblins stopped, looking nervous.

"So?" the one holding Lucky said rudely. "What's wrong with that?"

Rachel winked at Kirsty and Lara and then turned back to the goblins.

"Don't you know that's *doubly* unlucky?" she said, shaking her head. "You've really done it now!"

The goblins glanced at each other in dismay.

"Wh-what will happen now?" The third goblin gulped.

Kirsty shrugged. "Well, that's the thing with bad luck," she replied. "You never know what's going to happen!"

The goblins looked absolutely terrified.

"We don't want bad luck!" the one holding Lucky wailed. "How can we stop it?"

"Well, that's easy," Rachel said. "Just give us that black cat!"

"Yes, it's the only way to break the bad luck," Lara added. "And if you want to get some good luck back, there are lots of four-leaf clovers out in the field."

The goblins all frowned and stood there in silence for a moment. Kirsty, Lara, and Rachel waited anxiously to see what they would decide.

Would they give Lucky back?

Lucky at Last!

Finally, the three goblins nodded at one another.

"Let's go and get ourselves some good luck, and some for Jack Frost, too!" the goblin holding Lucky shouted. He put the little cat down on the floor and raced out of the barn. The other two goblins were right on his heels.

"They'll need all the good luck they can get when Jack Frost finds out they gave Lucky away!" Kirsty giggled.

"Yes, the goblins will need *hundreds* of lucky four-leaf clovers!" Rachel added with a grin.

Smiling from ear to ear, Lara held out her arms.

"Lucky!" she called.

The little cat's ears perked up. She bounded into the air and trotted right to Lara, shrinking down to fairy size with each step.

"Oh, it's so good to have

you back, Lucky!" Lara exclaimed,
gathering the cat into her arms and
giving her a big hug.

"*Meow!*" Lucky agreed, purring as
Rachel and Kirsty gently petted her
tiny, silky head.

"Girls, this is all thanks to you," Lara
announced gratefully. "I can't wait to
get back to Fairyland and tell everyone
how wonderful you both are! But
first . . ."

She waved her wand, and the cat
in Kirsty's arms became a tabby once
again. It blinked its eyes sleepily and
then began purring as it spotted Lucky.

"My magic has replaced the haystacks
in the farmyard, too," Lara told the
girls. "Now Lucky and I need to return
to Fairyland."

"Oh, no!" Rachel glanced at her watch, and then looked anxiously at Kirsty. "It's almost 12:30 and we haven't even started on our orienteering expedition!"

"Don't worry, girls," Lara winked at them. "I have a feeling everything will work out just fine."

She twirled her wand and a shower of fairy sparkles fell over herself and Lucky.

"Good-bye, girls, and thanks for everything!" Lara called as she and Lucky vanished.

"I was really worried that we weren't going to get Lucky back at all," Kirsty said, as she and Rachel hurried over to the barn door. "But we still managed to fool the goblins in the end!"

"Yes, we were *lucky*!" Rachel winked.

The girls walked out of the barn and then stopped in surprise. Outside stood Edward, their bunkmates, and all the other kids taking part in the orienteering expedition.

"Well, it looks like everyone found

our final meeting place!" Edward
remarked with a smile.

Kirsty and Rachel nodded, looking
relieved.

"Lara said everything would work out
fine—and it did!" Rachel whispered.

"We'll be doing some more orienteering after lunch," Edward said, "but first—the surprise!" He pointed at the pretty little farmhouse. "The farmer and his wife have invited us to lunch: fried chicken and corn on the cob, followed by fresh apple pie and ice cream! After that, they'll introduce us to some of the farm animals."

Everyone cheered, and Kirsty and Rachel grinned at each other.

"This is going to be great," Kirsty said happily. "And we've already had lots of fun today with Lara and Lucky!"

"Yes, every day is exciting when we're having fairy adventures!" Rachel agreed. "I wonder which amazing magical animal we'll meet next?"

RAINBOW magic

THE MAGICAL ANIMAL FAIRIES

Lara the Black Cat Fairy has
her magical animal back!
Now Rachel and Kirsty need to help

Erin
the Phoenix Fairy!

Join their next adventure
in this special sneak peek. . . .

Ha, Ha!

Kirsty Tate held her breath, trying to keep her fingers steady on the camera. A little brown sparrow stood only a few steps away, pecking at something on the ground. The bird was crouched at the edge of a forest clearing, framed by leafy trees and bushes, with sunlight shining through. Kirsty pressed the button on top

of the camera. *Click!* There—perfect.

"Fabulous," said her best friend, Rachel Walker, who was crouching next to Kirsty. She took her pencil and checked off the sparrow's picture on a list she held on a clipboard. "That makes five birds we've found and photographed," she said, feeling good. "The sparrow, thrush, blackbird, robin, and magpie. We just need the chickadee now, and we're done."

The two girls were spending a week of their spring break at an outdoor adventure camp. Today was Nature Day! All the campers had been put in pairs and given a list of plants, animals, or insects to track down and photograph. At the end of the day, they were going to gather around the

campfire and share their discoveries
with everyone.

Rachel and Kirsty sat down on a
fallen log to look at the birdwatcher's
guidebook they had been given. Rachel
flipped through until she found a page
about the chickadee. "Here we are," she
said, looking at the photograph. "So
it has a black head and throat, a short
bill, and a snowy white chest. Well, that
should be easy enough to spot."

"It says here that the chickadee is
acrobatic and clever, and has a funny
call: *chicka dee, dee, dee,*" Kirsty said,
reading aloud. She tilted her head to
one side. "I can't hear anything like
that," she said after a moment.

"I'll take a look with these," Rachel
said, picking up their binoculars and

scanning the glade. She moved them around slowly, spotting clumps of primroses and nodding daffodils, but no chickadees. The only bird she could see was a robin perched on a tree stump. Rachel giggled to herself as a joke suddenly popped into her head.

"What's so funny?" Kirsty asked.

"I just thought of a joke," Rachel said. "Which bird steals from the rich to give to the poor?"

"I don't know," Kirsty replied.

"Robin Hood!" Rachel giggled.

Kirsty smiled. "I've got one, too," she said. "Which bird tells the best jokes?"

Rachel shrugged. "I give up," she answered.

"A comedi-HEN!" Kirsty replied. Both girls laughed. . . .

RAINBOW magic™

SPECIAL EDITION

Three Books in Each One—
More Rainbow Magic Fun!

RAINBOW magic™

There's Magic in Every Series!

The Rainbow Fairies

The Weather Fairies

The Jewel Fairies

The Pet Fairies

The Fun Day Fairies

The Petal Fairies

The Dance Fairies

The Music Fairies

The Sports Fairies

The Party Fairies

The Ocean Fairies

The Night Fairies

The Magical Animal Fairies

Read them all!

◼ SCHOLASTIC

www.scholastic.com

www.rainbowmagiconline.com

HIT entertainment

RMFAIRY